Read about Greenbug's adventures when he takes a trip in his little engine. Greenbug's engine pulls a car transporter full of bug cars, Mr Frumble knocks a train off the track, Greenbug pulls a pickle train — and lots more! Don't forget to help Greenbug look for his friend Goldbug.

Richard Scarry's
Trains

Published in Great Britain with the authorization
of Winthers Forlag A/S by
World International Publishing Ltd., an Egmont Company,
Egmont House, PO Box 111, Great Ducie Street,
Manchester M60 3BL.
Printed in Germany. ISBN 0-7498-0429-7
REPRINTED 1992

Greenbug has a little engine.
He takes trips in it.
Everywhere he goes, he looks for his
friend, Goldbug.

Can you find
Goldbug in
each picture?

Greenbug leaves
the railway
station.

A freight train bumps its way along
a bumpy railway track.

Where is Goldbug?

The guard at the level crossing
lowers the gate.

Greenbug does not want to bump
into any cars crossing
the railway track.

Can you see Goldbug?

Greenbug sees a passenger train.
It passes by on another track.
Does he see Goldbug?

A worker loads
boxes of fruit
on to a wagon.

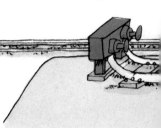

Greenbug's little engine pulls
a car transporter full of bug cars.
There are lots of kinds
of goods wagons.

Huckle Cat and Lowly Worm drive
their engine. The engine pulls
a guard's van.

Greenbug pulls a pickle train!

At the station people
buy food to eat.
Greenbug drives a
fruit train!

Oh, no! An engine jumps off the track. No one is hurt.

Mr Fixit comes along.
He will REALLY fix
the engine.
Look!

Oh, no!
Look what happens now.
The door of the wagon filled with
oranges comes open.

If Greenbug doesn't stop his engine
he will make a lot of orange juice!

Look out, Greenbug!
Don't run into the pickle wagon!

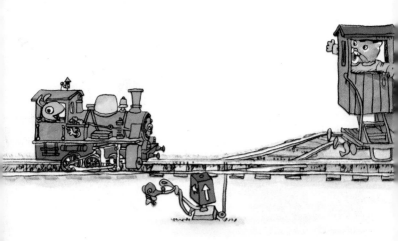

Just in time, he drives on to another track.

Greenbug arrives
at the station.

Look!
Mr Frumble drives his car into
the station and knocks a train
right off the track.
Don't worry.
Mr Fixit will fix it.

Choo, choo! Choo, choo!
Goodbye!